HERO

FREYA

STEVE BARLOW ✦ STEVE SKIDMORE
ART BY ANDREW TUNNEY

EDGE · FRANKLIN WATTS

Franklin Watts
First published in Great Britain in 2018
by The Watts Publishing Group

Text © Steve Barlow and Steve Skidmore 2018
Illustrations © Andrew Tunney 2018
Cover design: Peter Scoulding
Executive Editor: Adrian Cole

ISBN 978 1 4451 5237 0
ebook ISBN 978 1 4451 5238 7
Library ebook ISBN 978 1 4451 5239 4

1 3 5 7 9 10 8 6 4 2

Printed in Great Britain

MIX
Paper from
responsible sources
FSC® C104740
www.fsc.org

Franklin Watts
An imprint of
Hachette Children's Group
Part of The Watts Publishing Group
Carmelite House
50 Victoria Embankment
London EC4Y 0DZ

An Hachette UK Company
www.hachette.co.uk

www.franklinwatts.co.uk

How to be a Legend

Throughout the ages, great men and women have performed deeds so mighty that even though history has forgotten them, their names have passed into legend.

You could be one of them.

In this book, you are Freya, goddess of the Vikings. You must make decisions that will affect how the adventure unfolds.

Each section of this book is numbered. At the end of most sections, you will have to make a choice. The choice you make will take you to a different section of the book.

Some of your choices will help you to complete the adventure successfully. But choose carefully, some of your decisions could lead you into deadly danger!

If you fail, then start the adventure again and learn from your mistake.

If you choose wisely, you will succeed in your quest.

Are you ready to be a Hero? Have you got what it takes to become a Legend?

You are Freya, a young goddess of the Vikings. You live in Asgard, home of the gods.

One day, Odin, the father of the gods, summons you to his great hall, Valhalla. Thor, the god of thunder, stands beside him with his head held low.

Odin addresses you. "I want Thor to deal with a rebellion of the Frost Giants," says Odin, "but he has lost Mjolnir, his magic hammer, and with it all of his powers."

You bow. "I will find Mjolnir and return it to Thor."

Odin nods approvingly. Two crows fly down from a high beam and land on his shoulders. "My crows, Hugin and Munin, will spy out what is ahead of you and warn of danger," he says. "You have your magic falcon feather to fly unseen. And I shall give you a necklace of firestones that has the power to protect you and bind your enemies. If you are in mortal peril you must call on the Valkyries to rescue you. They will rewind time and bring you back to my hall."

You call for your chariot, drawn by two enormous cats, and set off at once in search of

Thor's magic hammer. With Odin's crows as your escort, you leave Asgard over Bifrost, the rainbow bridge that leads to Earth.

Go to 1.

1

As your chariot crosses over the rainbow bridge,
you see Loki, the trickster god, approaching.
You know that Loki is unreliable and not to be
trusted. Even so, he may know something that
can help you in your search.

If you wish to talk to Loki, go to 15.
If you wish to avoid Loki, go to 29.

You accept the lord's surrender, and ask if he has any news of Thor's hammer, but he knows nothing. You wonder why Loki has tried to hinder your quest.

You call on the firestones to return to their necklace form, and set off again to find the Norns.

The Norns are three beautiful, flaxen-haired women who decide the fates of men and women. They live beneath the great ash tree that holds up the sky. You find them in their longhouse, busy at the loom, weaving the tapestry that tells the history of the world. The threads that make up the tapestry are the fates of actual people.

They greet you cheerfully. "Freya! Just the goddess we most wanted to see! We're so tired of weaving — could you take over from us for a few minutes while we get something to eat and drink?"

If you are happy to accept and help the Norns, go to 17.

If you decide to refuse their request, go to 34.

3

"You're pretty bright, for a god," grumbles the dwarf. "You have earned the answers to two questions."

You think for a moment. "Where on Earth is Mjolnir?"

"It is not on Earth, but under it," replies the dwarf.

You stare at him. "What is that supposed to mean?"

The dwarf gives you a sly look. "Is that your second question?"

"No!" You rack your brains. "My second question is, who can lead me to Thor's hammer?"

The dwarf looks disappointed, but answers at once. "You must go to the Norns, who weave the fates of men ... oh, and women."

You leave the caverns of the dwarfs and return to your chariot.

Go to 33.

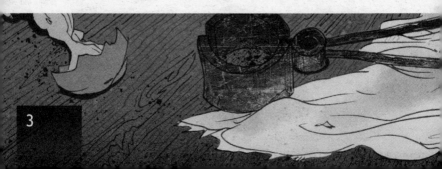

4

The Valkyries, warrior maidens who claim the spirits of those killed in battle, carry you through time and space, returning you to Valhalla.

Odin is not pleased to see you. "Perhaps I made a mistake in sending you," he says. "You're a young goddess — too inexperienced to deal with such a great matter."

You hang your head and promise to take more care in future.

"Very well," says Odin. "See that you do. The Frost Giants grow restless. There is no time to waste. Begin your quest again."

You remount your chariot and leave Asgard.

Choose more wisely next time! Go to 1.

5

"I cannot help you," you tell the dead.

The disappointed spirits set up a dismal wailing that attracts the attention of Nidhogg, the terrible serpent guardian of the dead. It belongs to Hel, their queen. The foul beast slithers towards you, fangs glistening with venom.

If you want to fight Nidhogg, go to 28.
If you want to surrender to Nidhogg and ask to be taken to Hel, go to 48.

6

"Thank you," you say. "That would be very welcome."

The lord shows you to a rich chamber, and orders his servants to bring you food and drink. Soon, you feel drowsy and fall asleep.

You wake to find yourself tied to the bed. Villagers are hurrying in carrying firewood and jars of oil. More wood is already stacked around you. They are planning to set fire to the bed!

You struggle against your bonds, but cannot break free. You have no choice but to call on the Valkyries for rescue.

The warrior maidens arrive, and cut through your bonds with their swords, before carrying you off to Valhalla and safety.

Go to 4.

7

With Hugin and Munin riding on your shoulders, you ride your chariot to the gates of Giantheim, the great palace of the giants.

You bang your fist on the door. "Open, in the name of Odin! I, Freya, command you!"

The doors open slowly. The hall is full of giants, who scowl at your arrogance. Slowly, and with discontented growls, they fall back to allow you to approach their lord.

If you decide to ask Thrym to help you find Mjolnir, go to 35.

If you decide to accuse Thrym of stealing Mjolnir, go to 49.

8

You raise your spear to attack, but before you can strike, Loki turns into a fly and your thrust misses him. You look around, but the trickster god is too small to see.

Then, hearing a noise behind you, you turn — but you are too late. Loki has now turned into a huge bear. He grabs you with his great arms; his powerful claws cut into you as he begins to crush you. You have barely enough breath to call upon the Valkyries for aid.

Go to 4.

9

Drawing your sword and axe, you leap into action. The dwarfs are small, but they are tough — and there seems to be an endless number of them! You are beaten back into the cave, and you realise that even if you defeat the dwarfs, you have no idea how to get out of their realm!

With no way out, you call on the Valkyries for help. They appear, shielding you from the dwarfs, and carry you back to Valhalla.

Go to 4.

10

The men and women stare at you with blank expressions. Then their mouths open wide, but no sound emerges. Instead, ghostly shapes pour out like mist; the shapes of animals which, as they touch the ground, become solid.

In moments, you are surrounded by bears, bulls, stags, boars and wolves. Eagles take off and circle overhead. You realise that this must be some enchantment cast by the lord of the village.

A wolf races to attack. You run it through with your spear; it howls in agony, and vanishes. At the same moment, you hear a terrible cry. The villager whose spirit formed the wolf falls to the ground, dead.

If you want to kill the other animals, go to 38.

If you decide you must find the lord, go to 47.

11

"You tried to kill me," you tell the lord. "For that, you must pay!"

You thrust your sword through the body of the fox. As it vanishes, the lord gives a howl of despair and falls to the ground, dead.

But the remaining villagers seem to gain new strength from the death of their lord. Their spirit animals surround you and close in, before attacking together...

There is no escape. You call on the Valkyries to bear you away.

Go to 4.

12

You send out Odin's crows to seek more news, and think about your next move. If Thrym is innocent, perhaps the dwarfs who forged Mjolnir can tell you something.

You set off for Darkheim, their underground realm. The dwarfs who meet you at the entrance to their caverns lead you through such a maze of passageways that you quickly become lost.

The chief dwarf is not in a welcoming mood. "The gods of Asgard are no friends of ours!" he grumbles. You start to question him about Mjolnir, but he shakes his head. "A question for an answer, that is the way of the dwarfs. I will ask you riddles. For each riddle you answer correctly, you are allowed one question."

You know dwarfs have no imagination – the riddles will be about something the chief dwarf can hear, see, smell, taste or touch at that moment.

If you want to accept the dwarf's terms, go to 46.

If you decide to refuse the contest, go to 32.

13

You race to attack – but Garm's thick hide turns aside your sword and spear, and his thick skull is too strong for your axe!

The great dog makes a frenzied assault. Even your armour is not sufficient protection from his ravening jaws. Under the ferocity of Garm's attack, you stumble and fall. Garm stands above you, ready to plunge his teeth into you. This is a fight you cannot win. You call upon the Valkyries to carry you to safety.

Go to 4.

14

"You have guessed one riddle," the dwarf says grandly, "so you are allowed to ask one question."

You take a deep breath. "Can you tell me who has the hammer?"

"No."

"Then who can?"

The dwarf shakes his head. "That's another question!"

"Would you like Odin to come down here and ask you himself?"

The dwarf decides not to push his luck. "Oh, all right! You must go to the Norns, who weave the fates of men ... and women."

You leave the caverns of the dwarfs and return to your chariot.

Go to 33.

15

You turn your chariot to meet Loki.

He looks up and sees you. A sneer spreads across his face. "Well met, little goddess! What do you want with me?"

You bite back an angry reply and tell him your quest.

Loki looks thoughtful. "The last time Mjolnir went missing, it was stolen by Thrym, lord of the giants."

You glare at Loki. Thrym once stole Mjolnir and would not return it unless you agreed to marry him. When you refused, Loki took Thor to Thrym, disguised as you. They recovered Mjolnir, but you found the whole business very embarrassing (though not as much as Thor did)!

Perhaps Loki is right, you think. Thrym might have stolen the hammer again. But would he be that foolish?

If you decide to go and find Thrym, lord of the giants, go to 43.

If you would rather ignore Loki, and continue your search for Mjolnir, go to 29.

16

You turn your back on Hel and make for the cave — but then you hear a slithering sound behind you. Too late, you remember that Hel has Nidhogg to do her bidding.

"Odin will never know you were here!" shrieks the queen of the dead. "Kill her, my beauty!"

If you wish to fight Nidhogg, go to 28.
To call upon the Valkyries for aid, go to 4.

17

"Gladly," you say.

You take over the Norns' work, weaving threads into the tapestry while they eat, drink and relax.

After a while, you ask them when they would like to return to their loom.

"Oh, no," they say. "You are doing it so well."

You grow angry. "I have no time to waste!" you tell the Norns. You try to leave the loom, but you cannot pull your fingers away from the threads.

The Norns laugh. "We are tired of all that hard work — you can do it for a change!"

If you wish to threaten the Norns, go to 44.
To try to trick them, go to 23.

18

"Fire!" you cry, thinking about the heat the dwarf can feel from the forge. The dwarf gives a cry of disappointed rage. "If you feed it with coal, it will burn — but if you poured your beer on it, it would go out."

The dwarf gnashes his teeth. "You have guessed the first riddle. But you will not guess the second!"

"Let us see," you say confidently. "Ask your riddle."

"Very well. The more I take, the more I leave behind. Tell me what I'm talking about."

If you think the answer is something the dwarf can see, go to 24.

If you think the answer is something the dwarf can hear, go to 41.

19

The Norns are furious at being tricked into taking up their work again. The eldest scowls at you. "You will pay for that, rash goddess!"

"That would not be just," you tell her calmly. "If I had acted without provocation, you would be right to punish me. But I only tricked you because you tried to trick me first. You cannot punish me for that. In any case, I am on a quest for Odin, and you tried to stop me from completing it. The All-father will be angry when he hears what you have done — unless you help me now."

The Norns mutter angrily, but they dare not defy Odin.

"Look in your tapestry," you tell the Norns. "Tell me who has Thor's hammer now, and where it can be found."

The Norns bend over their tapestry. "The god Loki has Mjolnir," says the eldest grudgingly. "He has taken it to the land of the dead; the realm of his daughter, Hel."

Go to 40.

20

"Thank you," you say, "but I will not rest in comfort until my quest is complete."

You set up camp in a nearby field, and fall asleep under the stars.

Some hours later, you awake to a sudden sense of danger. In the starlight, you see an axe hovering above you. Even though no one is holding the axe, it is raised and ready to strike!

If you wish to fight the axe with your sword, go to 45.

If you would rather use magic to protect you, go to 31.

21

You hold the magic feather aloft and transform into a falcon. With Odin's crows at your side, you swiftly fly to the giants' hall.

You fly in unnoticed through a high window, and you, Hugin and Munin search in every nook and cranny. Thor's missing hammer is nowhere to be found.

If you decide that Thrym does not have the hammer, and leave, go to 12.

If you want to return as Odin's messenger and confront Thrym, go to 7.

22

You turn away from Hel's gate and drive your chariot into a nearby forest. Here you hunt and kill a wild boar. You carry this on your shoulders to Garm's lair. As he sets about devouring it, you pass through the gates, telling Odin's crows to wait for you there.

The land of the dead is a seemingly endless, desolate grey plain, with the roots of the World Tree forming the "sky". You are surrounded by flies and the stench of corruption.

The spirits of the dead wander the land. They soon surround you, begging you to carry their messages to the living.

If you want to refuse their messages, go to 5.

If you want them to write down their messages, go to 36.

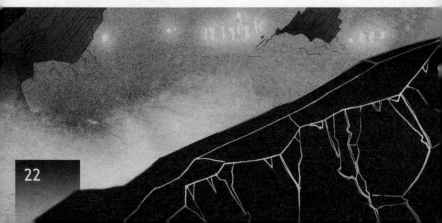

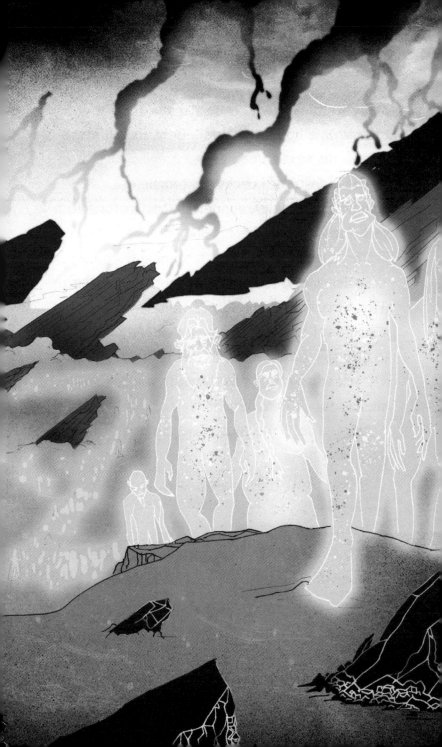

"Very well," you say. Then you stare at the tapestry as though puzzled. "Only, I can't see where this next thread goes."

The eldest Norn clicks her tongue in annoyance. "Foolish goddess! What's wrong with your eyes? It goes there!" She points at a place in the tapestry.

Deliberately, you position the thread in the wrong place. "What? Here?"

"No, no!" she reaches past you and begins to arrange the thread. "There!"

"And what about this thread?" you ask innocently. "I think it goes here..."

"Nonsense!" The second Norn snatches it from your hand. "It goes here..."

"And this thread?"

The youngest Norn takes it. "Here!"

As soon as all three Norns are busy showing you how to use the loom, you find your fingers are free of the spell. You step back quickly.

If you want to taunt the Norns, go to 30.
If you wish to question them, go to 19.

24

You look around. What can the dwarf see? "Candle!" you answer.

The dwarf howls with laughter. "And if I take the candle, I leave more behind? Talk sense!"

You curse your foolishness in giving the wrong answer.

If you guessed the first riddle correctly, go to 14.

If you got both answers wrong, go to 27.

25

You summon Hugin and Munin. "Guard her," you order.

Hel glares at you — but she knows the crows are Odin's pets. She dare not harm you while they are watching her.

You enter the cave Hel showed you, and find Loki casting spells over Thor's hammer. He turns and stares as you enter.

"So, you tried to put the blame on Thrym," you accuse, "when really, you were the thief!"

Loki snarls at you. "Beware, little goddess! When I have mastered the hammer's power,

I will be god of thunder, and Thor will be nothing!"

"You will have to fight me first," you tell him.

To attack Loki with your spear, go to 8.

If you would rather use the magic of the firestones against him, go to 42.

26

You attack the giants, and several of them fall.

But there are too many of them for you to overcome. First the sword, then the axe are wrenched from your hands. The firestone necklace is torn from your neck before you can call on its power. Odin's crows dive-bomb the giants, screeching and clawing, but their efforts are in vain. Soon you are a helpless prisoner.

Thrym is beside himself with fury. "Goddess or not," he roars, "you have insulted me. My giants will tear you to pieces!"

You have no choice but to call on the Valkyries to save you. A mighty wind rushes through the giants' hall. A dozen white swans appear. They transform into female warriors who surround you, and carry you away from danger.

Go to 4.

27

"You failed to guess the riddles, foolish goddess!" The dwarf dances around and clicks his fingers with glee. "Get out of my sight!"

You let your shoulders slump in defeat. You leave the head dwarf — but once out of sight, you straighten up with a gleam in your eye and slink back to listen outside his cave.

The dwarf is boasting of his victory. "Did you hear me bamboozle that stupid goddess?" he chortles. "Now she'll never know the only way she will get news of the hammer is to go to the Norns, who weave human fates!"

You creep away. Smiling inwardly, you ask the dwarf guards to show you out of their land. Maybe you're not so stupid, after all!

Go to 33.

28

You attack Nidhogg — but the serpent is too quick. Before you can get in even one spear thrust or sword cut, the terrible reptile has you gripped in its coils. Even as it squeezes the breath from your body, it prepares to plunge its venomous fangs into your neck.

Hel's pet is too much for you! You call upon the Valkyries to carry you to safety.

Go to 4.

29

You send out Odin's crows to search for Mjolnir. Meanwhile, you look high and low for Thor's hammer, in mountain, valley, lake and stream; but there is no sign of it.

Hugin and Munin appear and land on your shoulders.

"We have heard word that Mjolnir was last seen in the land of the giants."

You wonder whether to believe these rumours, but decide that you have no other leads to follow, and time moves on.

Go to 43.

30

You scoff at the Norns. "Who is foolish now? Silly women, slaves to your tapestry—"

You get no further. The eldest Norn's eyes seem to burn. "Insolent goddess. We are not slaves — we weave the fates of all! Would you like to see your own fate? Here it is!"

The tapestry tears itself from the loom and flies at you like some great multicoloured bird. It engulfs you, weaving you into its threads. You feel yourself dissolving into the substance of the tapestry. While you still have a voice, you call upon the Valkyries for help.

Go to 4.

31

You take the necklace and hurl it towards the enchanted axe.

The necklace hangs, spinning, in the air. A golden glow surrounds it as it transforms into a shield. The axe attacks — but cannot break the shield — until it drops to the earth, its magic spent.

You call your cats to harness them to the chariot. You go to pick up the magical shield, but as you do, you hear stealthy sounds all around. Villagers appear from all directions, holding flaming torches. You are surrounded.

Go to 10.

32

You angrily refuse the dwarf's offer. "I am the representative of Odin! You risk the wrath of Asgard if you do not tell me what I want to know!"

The dwarf scowls. "You are not in Asgard now, Miss High and Mighty!" He gives a piercing whistle. Well-armed dwarfs appear from the shadows brandishing axes, spears and crossbows.

If you want to fight the dwarfs, go to 9.

If you would rather submit and agree to the riddle contest, go to 46.

33

As your chariot takes you towards the house of the Norns, you realise that your travels have made you hungry and thirsty.

You arrive at a village, and seek food and shelter. But the men and women of the village are sullen and reserved, and will not talk to you.

"Please excuse them." A man in fine-looking clothes appears. "They are superstitious peasants, and not used to dealing with a goddess such as yourself."

The man introduces himself as the lord of the village, and offers you accommodation in his hall. You sense a powerful magic aura coming from the lord. This man is a magician; you are not sure whether to trust him.

If you wish to accept the lord's offer, go to 6.

If you would rather refuse it, go to 20.

34

"My business is urgent," you say. "I have no time..."

Before you can finish your sentence, the beautiful Norns instantly transform into fearsome hags. "Worthless goddess!" they cry. "Learn that fate can be kind, but it can also be cruel!"

The Norns' fingers fly over the tapestry. Plagues of biting and stinging insects fly from it, and surround you. Snakes and scorpions slither and scuttle from beneath the loom to attack you.

No one — mortal or god — can fight their fate. With the last of your strength, you call on the Valkyries for help.

Go to 4.

35

You explain about the missing hammer and ask for the giants' assistance.

Thrym replies courteously, "Truly, I do not know what has become of Thor's hammer."

To accept Thrym's word and leave, go to 12.

If you decide that Thrym is lying and want to accuse him, go to 49.

36

The spirits look around — but there is nothing in the dead land to write their messages with, or on! While they make hopeless attempts to write messages in the sand or on dead leaves, you slip away and walk on until you arrive at the palace. You know that Hel lives here with her terrible pet, Nidhogg, the fearsome serpent-guardian of the dead.

Go to 48.

37

You stare at the things the dwarf is eating and drinking. "Beer!" you cry.

The dwarf laughs. "Wrong!"

"Meat, then!"

"You're only allowed one guess!" The dwarf grins. "Wrong again, anyway. The answer is 'fire'; if I feed it with coal, it will burn — but if I pour beer on it, it will go out."

You bite your lip. You know you must do better. "Ask your second riddle," you tell the dwarf.

"Very well, although it hardly seems worth bothering, given your last attempt. Answer me this, young goddess: the more I take, the more I leave behind. Tell me what I'm talking about."

If you think the answer is something the dwarf can see, go to 24.

If you think the answer is something the dwarf can hear, go to 41.

38

You attack with axe and sword. More animals fall and vanish, and every time one does, a villager shrieks and drops to the ground.

But you are faced with many powerful creatures. Eagles claw at your head. You try to escape in your chariot, but a pack of wolves attacks your cats and it overturns, throwing you out. As you lie stunned on the grass, bears seize you in their terrible claws, and bulls and boars rush in to finish you...

With your last breath, you call on the Valkyries for help. Instantly, they appear in shimmering armour and carry you out of this time and place to safety.

Go to 4.

Sword dancing, axe whirling, you advance
on Thrym.

Some of the other giants standing around
move in to protect him, but Thrym angrily
waves them back. "Let no one interfere!
I fight my own battles!"

You join in combat. The giant is strong,
but you are a goddess. The power of Asgard
strengthens your arm, and the necklace of
firestones protects you. Soon, Thrym lies helpless
at your feet, with your sword at his throat.

"Thief!" you cry. "Your life is forfeit!"

Thrym glares at you. "Take my life if you
wish," he snarls, "but I am no thief! I know
nothing of Thor's hammer!"

You realise that the giant is telling the truth.
You have achieved nothing by fighting; you have
only made an enemy. You agree to spare Thrym
in return for safe passage out of his realm.

Go to 12.

40

You take to your chariot again, just as Odin's crows rejoin you.

"We have found no trace of Mjolnir," caws Hugin.

"Then come with me," you tell them. "I know where the hammer is."

With Hugin and Munin flying at your shoulders, you reach the gates of Hel's gloomy kingdom, the land of the dead.

Guarding the gates is Hel's pet, a giant dog called Garm. He doesn't like visitors — especially ones who arrive in a chariot pulled by cats! He snarls and growls at you; he obviously does not intend to let you past.

If you want to fight Garm, go to 13.

If you would rather try to pacify Garm, go to 22.

41

"I can hear dwarfs hurrying outside your cave," you tell the chief dwarf. "The more steps they take, the more distance they leave behind. The answer is — footsteps!"

The dwarf stamps his feet and tears at his beard in disappointed rage.

If you answered both riddles correctly, go to 3.

If you answered only this one correctly, go to 14.

42

You tear the necklace from your throat and hurl it at Loki.

The necklace opens out, becoming a glowing rope that winds itself around the trickster god, pinning his arms and legs, rendering him helpless in a heartbeat. Loki is at your mercy, and Thor's hammer is yours to claim.

Go to 50.

43

You wonder whether you should take your chariot and go to Thrym, lord of the giants, on an official visit as a messenger from Asgard. Or should you use your magic falcon feather to transform into a hawk, and spy out the land first?

If you decide to take the chariot, go to 7.
To use the feather, go to 21.

44

"Let me go!" you cry, "or you will feel the edge of my sword and the weight of my axe!"

The Norns laugh scornfully. "Poor goddess, but you cannot take your hands from the tapestry."

You realise the Norns intend to keep you weaving for a long time — perhaps forever! There is only one way to escape them — you call upon the Valkyries to come and save you.

Go to 4.

45

You draw your sword and take guard. But as soon as the axe descends, your sword shatters. The axe is an enchanted weapon, and no blade can withstand a blow from it! The lord of the village is clearly a powerful magician. The axe attacks you again.

If you wish to call on the Valkyries to help you, go to 4.

If you want to use magic to protect you, go to 31.

46

You realise that you cannot force the dwarf to tell you what he knows — without his help, you cannot even find your way out of the caves!

"I agree," you say. The dwarf cackles and rubs his hands.

You look around the cave. The dwarf is sitting beside a blazing forge that smells of hot metal. He is eating meat and drinking beer by the light of a candle. On his lap lies a war-axe around whose handle he has been binding gold thread. The sounds of hurrying feet and shouted conversations of dwarfs going about their business outside the cave echo around its stone walls.

The dwarf gives you a nasty grin. "Here is my

first riddle. Feed me and I live; give me a drink and I die," he says. "What am I?"

If you think the answer is something the dwarf can feel, go to 18.

If you think the answer is something he can taste, go to 37.

47

You fend the creatures off as best you can, trying not to kill them. Looking around, you see a fox standing on its hind legs, yelping, and pointing with its front paws. It seems to be directing the attack.

You use your magic shield to batter a path through the press of attackers. The fox is so busy organising its followers, it fails to see you until the last minute. It tries to run, but you are too quick. You catch the creature and threaten it with your sword.

The lord of the village appears. "Please, spare my spirit!"

"Why did you attack me?" you demand.

"The god Loki appeared to me in a vision and told me you had vowed to destroy my magic. I offer you my friendship and gifts if you will leave my village in peace."

If you wish to accept the lord's surrender, go to 2.

If you would rather kill the lord's spirit, go to 11.

48

You find Hel awaiting you. She is a strange and dreadful goddess. Above the waist, she appears to be a beautiful woman, but her lower half is that of a rotting corpse.

"What do you want, little Freya?" she sneers.

"I want Thor's hammer," you tell her.

Hel looks angry and guilty at the same time. "I know nothing of Mjolnir!"

"I have been sent by Odin himself," you say.

Now Hel looks scared. "I want no trouble from the All-father." She points to a nearby cave. "You will find what you seek in there."

If you want to head straight for the cave, go to 16.

If you want to call Odin's crows to guard Hel, go to 25.

49

You draw your sword and war-axe. "You are lying!" you tell Thrym. "Thor's hammer is here!"

Thrym rises from his throne, enraged. The other giants in the hall mutter angrily and reach for their weapons.

If you want to attack the giants, go to 26.
If you want to attack Thrym, go to 39.

50

You return to Asgard and hand the bound and furious Loki to Odin. Then you return Mjolnir to its rightful owner.

Thor is delighted and promises to use his hammer to defeat your enemies.

"Those Frost Giants won't know what hit them," you say.

Thor brandishes Mjolnir. "Oh, yes, they will!"

Odin thanks you. "You have saved Asgard. I predict that one day, you will be the greatest goddess among us. You are already a hero — and a legend!"

HERO
LEGENDS
HERCULES
EDGE
STEVE BARLOW · STEVE SKIDMORE
ART BY ANDREW TUNNEY

You are Hercules, a hero living in ancient Greece. You are known for your great strength and courage. You have had many adventures, fighting and defeating monstrous creatures, such as the nine-headed hydra and the Nemean lion.

The goddess Hera hates you and is always trying to place you in perilous situations, which she hopes you will not survive. Luckily, the goddess Athene likes you and helps you avoid Hera's traps.

As part of your latest adventure, you and Hylas, your arms-bearer, have joined the crew of the Argo to help another hero, Jason, in his quest to find the Golden Fleece. With the other Argonauts, you have spent days at sea, battling the storms created by Hera's brother, Poseidon, god of the sea...

Continue the adventure in:
IHERO LEGENDS
HERCULES

About the 2Steves

"The 2Steves" are
Britain's most popular
writing double act
for young people,
specialising in comedy
and adventure. They
perform regularly in schools and libraries,
and at festivals, taking the power of words
and story to audiences of all ages.

Together they have written many books,
including the *I HERO Immortals* and *iHorror* series.

About the illustrator:
Andrew Tunney (aka 2hands)

Andrew is a freelance artist and writer based in
Manchester, UK. He has worked in illustration, character
design, comics, print, clothing and live-art. His work
has been featured by Comics Alliance, ArtSlant Street,
DigitMag, The Bluecoat, Starburst and Forbidden Planet.
He earned the nickname "2hands" because he can draw
with both hands at once. He is not ambidextrous; he just
works hard.

Also in the I HERO Legends series:

ATHENA
Steve Barlow · Steve Skidmore
Art by Andrew Tunney

978 1 4451 5234 9 pb
978 1 4451 5235 6 ebook

BEOWULF
Steve Barlow · Steve Skidmore
Art by Andrew Tunney

978 1 4451 5225 7 pb
978 1 4451 5226 4 ebook

KING ARTHUR
Steve Barlow · Steve Skidmore
Art by Andrew Tunney

978 1 4451 5231 8 pb
978 1 4451 5232 5 ebook

ROBIN HOOD
Steve Barlow · Steve Skidmore
Art by Andrew Tunney

978 1 4451 5183 0 pb
978 1 4451 5184 7 ebook

Have you read the I HERO Atlantis Quest mini series?

MENACE FROM THE DEEP
Steve Barlow · Steve Skidmore

978 1 4451 2867 2 pb
978 1 4451 2868 9 ebook

OCEAN ALLIANCE
Steve Barlow · Steve Skidmore

978 1 4451 2870 2 pb
978 1 4451 2871 9 ebook

BATTLE FOR THE SEAS
Steve Barlow · Steve Skidmore

978 1 4451 2876 4 pb
978 1 4451 2877 1 ebook

ATLANTIS ASSAULT
Steve Barlow · Steve Skidmore

978 1 4451 2873 3 pb
978 1 4451 2874 0 ebook

Also by the 2Steves...

978 1 4451 4081 0 pb
978 1 4451 4082 7 eBook

You are the last Dragon Warrior.
A dark, evil force stirs within the
Iron Mines. Grull the Cruel's
army is on the march! YOU must
stop Grull.

978 1 4451 4088 9 pb
978 1 4451 4087 2 eBook

You are a noble mermaid —
your father is King Edmar.
The Tritons are attacking your home
of Coral City. YOU must save the Merrow
people by finding the Lady of the Sea.

978 1 4451 4084 1 pb
978 1 4451 4085 8 eBook

You are Olympian, a superhero.
Your enemy, Doctor Robotic,
is turning people into mind slaves.
Now YOU must put a stop to his
plans before it's too late!

978 1 4451 3958 6 pb
978 1 4451 3961 6 eBook

You are a young wizard.
The evil Witch Queen has captured
Prince Bron. Now YOU must rescue
him before she takes control of
Nine Mountain kingdom!